A Working Housewife

THE ONE WHO NEVER RETIRES

SHALBHA SINGH

First Published in March 2020

ISBN: 978-93-90034-75-8

BLUEROSE PUBLISHERS

www.bluerosepublishers.com

info@bluerosepublishers.com

+91 8882 898 898

Cover Design:

Tyngshain Pariat

Typographic Design:

Namrata Saini

Distributed by: BlueRose, Amazon, Flipkart, Shopclues

Acknowlegment

Well, it was much easier for me to just thank everyone associated with me and save my energy but it wouldn't be justified. A few people deserve special mention as this book is and will always be closest to my heart. It was undoubtably impossible without the blessings of my parents and teachers who made me what I am today.

I would like to express my gratitude towards my good friend Miss. Aparajita Jamwal currently a practising advocate at High Court of Jammu and Kashmir, who not only recklessly lent her time to come up with the idea of writing a book , also encouraged me to write the book to provide an outlet for my feelings while I was grieving on my mother's untimely demise.

I would like to thank my elder sister Dr. Shailja Singh currently practising as a Dentist at Raipur, Chhattisgarh who tried her level best to help me but couldn't provide satisfactory help.

I would like to thank all my friends who have always supported me no matter what like my own family right from childhood till today.

I would also like to thank BlueRose publishers who helped me to portray a beautiful picture of my thoughts by helping me in publishing my first ever book. Their team not only published my book but also encouraged me to go for it even when I was a newbie.

Dedication

“Dedicated to all the mothers who have been contributing to the society by being a housewife.”

Preface

Everyone has a special place of a mother in their life and like everyone even I shared a unique bond with my mother too. Most of the incidents recorded in this book are my personal experiences with her or the one narrated by her. I know there will always be a scarcity of words to express the greatness of a mother. But, through this book I am trying to show you a glimpse of an ordinary woman with extraordinary will power, altruistic attitude, love and greatness.

Unfortunately, I lost my mother at an early age but I still live every moment cherishing her teachings and experiences, which she shared with me. In this book, I have tried to cover her entire life right from her childhood till her sad demise, but the message I intent is to all the housewives in the world who are not given due credence of their work, to value their contribution to the society.

The Author

SHALBHA SINGH

Contents

An act of God 1
The Great Indian annoying wedding 6
An unwavering will power 8
A big blow to dowry 10
A kosher custody 12
The withering 16
Embarking on a new role 18
Acceptance of the moment 20
An astonishing turn 22
A stroll towards infinity 24
A selfless voyage 26
Mastering a sorcerer's spell 28
The hopeful spirit 30
The silence reminds me of you 32
The smiling face 34

An act of God

Born in the kingdom of lions,
Raised like a lioness among them all,
A breezy laughter and virtuous soul,
To be a human being was her only goal.

Transformed the belief of the patriarch,
A daughter crowned as a monarch,
A sister to three brothers,
With a consistent endeavour to earn feathers.

A girl who was good at every game,
To her, studies and household work were an easy game,
Theatre and dancing were not only for fame,
Mastering all trades was her passion to tame.

A beloved daughter of her father,
A beloved sister of her brothers,
A beloved wife of her husband,
A beloved mother of her children.

My mother Late Mrs.Rita Singh was born in a typical Rajput family on 4 December 1964. Her father Late Shri Jaikaran Singh was a sales tax officer and mother Late Shrimati Shantidevi Singh was a housewife. She had three brothers and was the second child. She was married to Shri Ashok Kumar Singh, a forest officer. As a wife, she was a great partner and would involve herself in all of her partner's pursuits. Being an expert in home management, she was known for her hospitality.

Like a tigress, she fiercely protected her children. Also, she didn't mind turning into one when she had to discipline her children or deal with her husband. It would be extremely unjust to say that she was blessed with two daughters and one son; instead, we were abundantly blessed to have her as our mother.

She was a very active lady throughout her life who gave and commanded respect & love from everyone around her. She excelled in so many things and always had a burning desire in her to learn more and more. I don't remember I have ever seen her sitting wasting time. She excelled not only at academics but at cooking too. She knew how to make more than 200 types of sauces and pickles. In fact, she was once offered to supply her pickles to a resort owned by family friends situated at Bandhavgarh, but she delivered it for free.

I would like to share her a few achievements which fortunately are still intact with me.

The following is a list of her achievements:

Six-months diploma in computers from Aptech Institute

One-year diploma in Ayurveda from Maharshi Mahesh Yogi University

1997 – MA in English Literature from Awadhesh Pratap Singh University

1988 – BSc in Botany/Zoology/Chem/General English

1984– Won the first place at a science exhibition during Master of Science, held at Government Girls Higher Secondary School Rewa, Madhya Pradesh

1984 – Won the first place for Pre-English drama during her Master of Science. Special certificate as a co-star Government Girls higher Secondary School

1980 – Was a table tennis player at Sagar Division

1978 – Played the role of Shakuntala at Mahakavi Kalidas Samaroh held at Sagar Division

1977 – Won the third place in long jump at P.K. School, Rewa

1977 – Won the first place in 100 m race at P.K. School, Rewa

1977 – Division level player of Basketball at Sagar

1977–78 –Was awarded 2 Stars by the Government of India Ministry of Education and Social Welfare for participating in National physical efficiency tests.

1972 – Won the third place at St. Norberts Girls Higher Secondary School, Jabalpur

1970 – Won the third place in the debate competition hosted by District Cooperative Society Ltd. at Sagar

Science exhibition the one who is explaining

First from the left

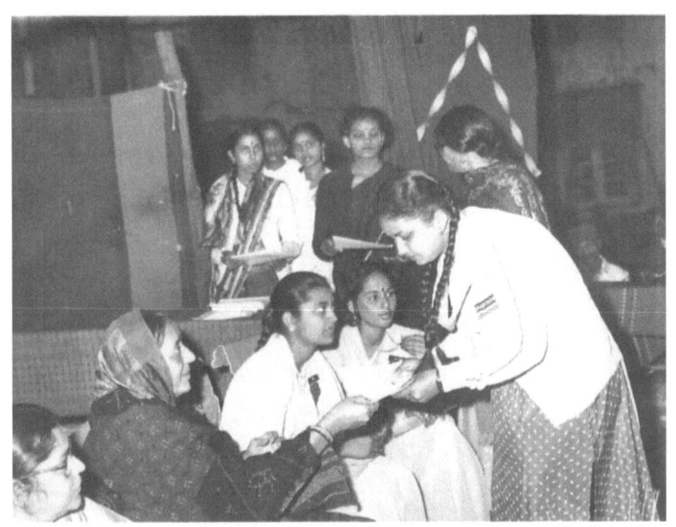

The one receiving certificate

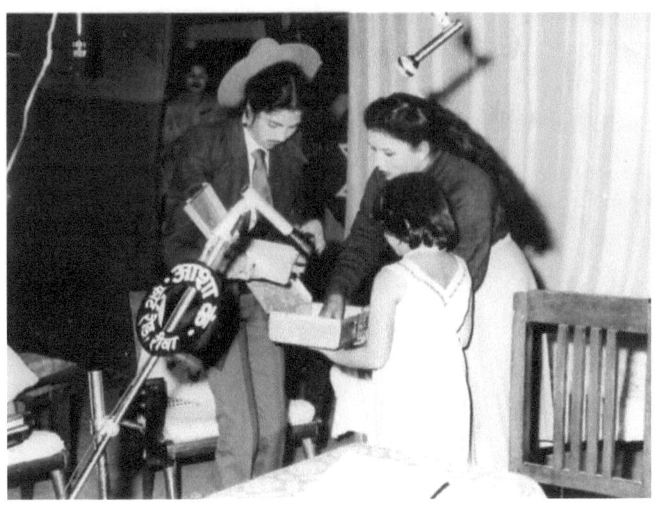

English drama the one with open hair

The Great Indian annoying wedding

You are my angel,
You are so cute,
You are so adorable,
You are the most beautiful.

Parents were her only mirror,
And mirrors never lie was her staunch belief,
But then the belief shattered,
When she was seen as a daughter-in-law

The abode of happiness in her eyes,
Was drowned in a flood of tears,
Suddenly the priceless feathers,
Transformed into a frozen mass of ridicule.

My mother excelled at many things, but it wasn't sufficient to please a bridegroom's family. During her childhood, she was not fair as per the Indian norms of marriage. Her neighbour constantly taunted her that although she is good at everything, she would still not get a handsome husband because she weighed more than average girls then and dark skinned.

She had narrated this story to me on several occasions. She always advised me to never let anyone make me ashamed of my body. After having taught me so, she was once complaining about my looks. I told her that it is because I got my looks from her and not Aishwarya Rai. Had it been she, my mother, I wouldn't have had to listen to this. I was graciously kicked out by my mother from the couch on which we both were sitting.

An unwavering will power

Her unwavering spirit of excellence,
Shone everywhere she went,
Her uncanny resemblance to the pertinacious waves,
Worn out even the most unformidable of them all.

The ugly figure in the mirror,
As perceived by the society,
Could not combat,
With her all-enduring iron will.

Her charisma continued to suffuse,
Undermining the ego of the mirror,
A women as virtuous as holy truth,
Belittled the phony kingdom of beauty.

My mother did not lose her willpower even after being body shamed and excelled in every field, mindless of other people's opinions. She fostered her exuberant energy in me and always advised me to never let others judge my beauty. She consistently inculcated various skills in us, such as dancing, karate, cooking, stitching, and painting, because of her staunch belief that talents will always transcend looks.

She did not give credence to the stereotypical role of women in the kitchen, but still taught us to cook, because she believed that 'Wherever you go, your stomach goes along. So, you should know to cook'.

During her illness also she always had one or the other plan to celebrate each and every day.

A big blow to dowry

Once again, a bride was weighed in Gold
Once again, the soul of human being
Was asphyxiated by the weight of Gold
Once again, the doors were closed for a poor.

A 12-year-old with an iron resolution,
Wanted to break this tradition and stood against all odds,
The fearless lioness roared persistently,
And her words pierced and echoed throughout the crowd.

Her father was her hero,
Alas! his valour tumbled before her eyes,
When she realised he was a part of the feather-brained crowd,
She reminded him that, one day, his daughter will also be a bride.

When the elders in my mother's village were planning to cancel her one of the cousins' marriage due to insufficient dowry, at that time she was probably in her middle school. Her silent nature turned violent on seeing her own father sitting with those who were in favour of rejecting the alliance. She couldn't stop herself and crushed them with her mighty words. She asked her father to empathise with the situation. Finally, she won over the crowd, including her father, who then agreed for the marriage. All the older ladies in her family started crying and hugging her for her tenacity.

A kosher custody

Ornaments were meant to be just metal,
Her only pride were her values,
Renowned for her virtuousness,
With an unimpeachable integrity, she fought for others.

One of her ornaments was her impeccable trust,
Intransient to even a volcanic threat,
One of the adornments which made her personality glare,
Breaking somebody's trust even she couldn't dare.

During her college days when mom was staying at a hostel, her relative sent her daughter to the same hostel and asked my mother to look out for her. Later, the girl was involved with a married professor who exploited her. Mom revealed this incident to the girl's father who consequently removed the girl from the hostel. The best part was, after ruining that girl's fantasy, mom also attended her wedding later in her life and wished her a happy and prosperous married life.

A river is fearless for its own selfish needs,
For a rendezvous with the sea,
A tiger is fearless for its own selfish ends,
For killing and bringing a life to an end.

Countless selfish ends to be met,
But she was fearless to raise her voice for herself and for others,
A river could change its course and be wise,
But she faced it all without even blinking her eyes.

There was a married professor in her college who used to always flirt with female students. He was once fooling around with her friend and was cheating on his wife. When she came to know about it, she first scolded her friend and then the professor, without caring about the consequences. She even risked her practical marks for final exams in which he played a crucial role.

The withering

A gardener showed a dream,
To a blooming bud,
That she is going to be,
For ever and ever.

The poor bud didn't know,
That it will be the gardener,
Who will choose,
To sever her from her abode.

It was not a drop of mist,
It was the bud's tears,
But the gardener chose to believe,
It was the fate of the bud from which it cannot be relieved.

Everyone saw the blooming bud,
And thought it to be the happiest,
But nobody noticed,
That the bud was forced to accept the fate.

Mom was studying for master's in chemistry when one fine day, she was informed of her arranged marriage. She wanted to build her career, but she was not given an option and was asked to get ready for her marriage on 8 May 1984 to a guy from Sidhi district. I recall my maternal grandmother telling me that mom initially, was very angry as she thought a guy from Sidhi will stand where in life but later when she was told that he is a forest officer and she saw his photograph, her anger was gone. She cried every day until she got married because this wasn't her plan. She wanted to first get a good job and then get into a married life.

Embarking on a new role

The myth was broken,
And the truth of the mirror was revealed,
The princess found a prince,
Mocking the mirror.

Her union with the prince,
Was welcomed with a celebration,
But what everyone ignored,
Was the shattering sound of her dreams.

Although she was mocked for her looks during her childhood, she found an extremely handsome forest officer as her partner. To everyone's surprise, her father-in-law—being too principled—had fixed the marriage on the basis of her academic achievements, without considering her looks. Though she had seen her partner's photograph, he saw hers only a few days before the wedding. Everyone enjoyed the wedding, but she did not. She accepted & respected her father's desire and got ready for the marriage, but she wasn't happy as all her dreams to have a career first shattered into pieces. That was one thing she always told us and did everything to make us achieve education and economic independence.

Acceptance of the moment

A cloud cloaks the raindrops,
In its arms tightly,
And then releases them,
As if it is meant to be.

Every stage of life had its own challenge,
Facing the challenge was an easy task,
But facing the daunting challenge with a smile,
Was a facile venture for her.

A daughter had proved,
That she was no less than a son,
A woman had proved,
That she can play a myriad of roles.

Without knowing the destiny of any drop,
The cloud bids goodbye to it,
The drop's fate may be to land as a drop on a leaf,
But it is capable of turning into an ocean.

My mother got married on 8 May 1984 to an under-training forest officer. Her father was a sales tax officer and led a wealthy life. Because he had lost his parents at the age of 10 years, he wanted to provide all the luxuries to his children. She sometimes told us the differences of our times reminiscing that she had the liberty to wear miniskirts and owned a high-end bicycle at an age when my sister and I wore salwar-suits. She found it amusing sometimes to tease us by comparing her father to ours.

Mom's married life was totally different from how she lived before marriage. The house was under construction, and there were still doors to be fitted. The money saved by her partner for starting their married life was stolen during the marriage ceremony. Her husband got first posted in Mandla, Madhya Pradesh and their household utensils consisted of a plate, bowl, tumbler, cooker and a wok. I recall her narrating an incident where she had to offer a guest, drinking water in a bowl because she didn't have two tumblers. This was the situation she had to deal with after marriage. Being a down-to-earth person, she endured it all calmly. She even had to cook in an earthen stove (Chulha), which she was unfamiliar with.

An astonishing turn

The moment she merged with the ocean,
The river thought that it is her end,
What she did not realise was,
It is a new start.

After being plucked from the plant,
The flower thought that it is her end,
What it did not realise was,
It is a new start.

When it shed all its leaves,
The tree thought that the autumn is its end,
What it did not realise was,
It is a new start.

Immediately after her marriage, she sunk into depression convinced that it is the end of her career and life. To her surprise, it was just the beginning. Post marriage, her partner encouraged her to write entrance exams for medicals. Her husband supported her in all her endeavours such as pursuing courses in computers and completing her master's in English while raising three children. I distinctly remember her sitting on a chair with a whip to scare us (her own three children along with their six cousins) into sleep, as the house was in utter chaos all thanks to us. One fine day, she vowed never to hit us, but I managed to have her break her vow the same evening.

A stroll towards infinity

Ignorant of self,
A new life,
Joined the race of living beings.

Ignorant of the real journey,
A new life,
Started its journey.

Ignorant of the purpose of life,
A new life,
Blindly walked the path constructed by others.

Ignorant of the union with a companion,
A new life,
Realised that the real journey is the journey within self.

Ignorant of the ultimate end,
A new life,
Started cherishing the path towards it.

Although mom believed in God, she had never followed the rituals religiously before she got married. However, her life partner was quite a religious person. After her enlightenment in 1998, she became so religious that she fasted for almost three days a week and read a lot of religious scriptures. She started attending numerous religious congregations (Satsang) and became engrossed in meditation.

One of her major achievements was the Narmada parikrama in a Marshal Jeep, accompanied by her husband and the priests of the Narmada temples in Amarkantak, a town located in Madhya Pradesh from where the river Narmada originates. During that time, her health was poor, but she started off her journey from Amarkantak, Madhya Pradesh and ended it in Gujrat. During the entire journey, she slept on the floor, stayed only in ashrams, and cooked her own food along with the priests of Narmada temples. Each day, at the crack of dawn, Rudrabhishek was performed, and she participated every time despite her poor health.

A selfless voyage

Natural it is to be happy with one's own existence,
Wanting more for only oneself,
Leaving no room in mind and heart,
To consider other's struggle.

Natural it was for her,
To consider other's hunger as hers,
To immerse others' tears into hers,
To belittle her own pain before other's sorrows.

The hand that fed her fed others,
The hand that wiped her tears wiped other's tears too,
The celebration of bliss within herself,
Was only relished when she comforted the unheard.

It was her belief that social service starts at home. Hence, she laid down a rule in the house that whatever is cooked for her family shall be shared with the helpers too. She was always enthusiastic to help others in every possible manner and considered their troubles as her own. She always found ways to hold enormous feasts for the helpers' families too, for example, by celebrating her children's birthdays and inviting all the helpers and their families along with her friends and family. Distributing blankets or presenting her own shawl to a needy was no big deal for her. Materialistic pleasure held no meaning for her compared with being a reason for other's happiness. She always took the lead in helping a poor family to get their daughter married.

Mastering a sorcerer's spell

No one taught the birdie to build her nest,
No one taught the seed to grow into a tree,
No one taught the raindrop to create an ocean,
No one taught a flame to wipe the darkness.

No one taught a mother to knit the future of her child,
No one taught the earth to build an abode for living,
The creator at his best,
Using the sorcery of creation,
Soaked her soul,
With the magical spell to create.

My mother was also an artist. She knew nib, clay, and tie and dye painting; stitching; thread art; and knitting. Once her husband was posted at Kanker, a remote location (at the time in Madhya Pradesh, currently in Chhattisgarh), and he couldn't arrive home for Rakshabandhan (a festival of siblings where a sister ties a talisman around her brother's wrist and the brother vows to protect his sister from all harms). Since money in cash was only used for transaction and her husband was unable to reach home, there was insufficient money to buy threads for talisman (rakhi). I recall that late at night, she suggested using acrylic threads to make rakhis by making a bow and then rubbing it with a toothbrush at its tips. She even taught her daughter and her neighbour's daughter to make beautiful nib paintings. Since she was good at knitting, she knitted all our woollen clothes till we were out of our school days.

The hopeful spirit

The sculptor gave hope,
To the object lying in despair,
That it will be praised of its beauty,
After enduring this extreme pain.

The connoisseur gave hope,
To the broken and shattered rock,
That it will shine like a diamond,
Amidst all the darkness.

The musician gave hope,
To the crying broken string,
That it will be cherished,
As the most melodious sound.

She gave hope,
To the sinking breath of hope,
That it is capable of rising,
Like a tide by her words.

Mom was an iron-willed woman. She had her own style of boosting others' confidence. When her son had met with a fatal accident and was in coma for more than 15 days, her husband had lost all hope, but she was optimistic. I recall her determined voice, 'Nothing will happen to my son, he will be fine in sometime'. It was her faith that helped her son recover in no time.

I wasn't able to keep up with the competition during my 12th standard board exams and lost all hope. When the time for results was close, she said, 'Haanthi kitna bhi dubla hoga lekin gadha kabhi nahi hoga', meaning however much an elephant loses weight, he would never become a donkey. To my surprise, I cleared the exam with flying colours, with exactly the same percentage which she predicted.

Mom not only boosted confidence in others but was self-confident too. She had almost three heart attacks and unfortunately succumbed to death the fourth time. My father and me were her constant companions during hospital visits. I fondly recall that even during that time, she was always ready for an adventurous trip. She was so meticulous that even on the hospital bed, after she gained consciousness, she strictly ensured that her hair were oiled and well-pleated. She took her own medicines on time without even being reminded and also had every possible thing forbidden to eat for which she was constantly reminded.

The silence reminds me of you

The waves of the blue clamour,
But the crusade with silence is forever,
The victory of the wailing silence is not veiled,
Sometimes, the sonance of silence cannot be braced.

The souls of the nomadic ricers maundered,
But the curse of quiescence spares never,
The triumph of the fatal quiescence is not cloaked,
Sometimes the turbulent quiescence cannot be endured.

The troops of raindrops march leaving ivory abode,
But the insatiable thirst of earth is never ignored,
The conquest of the thirst cannot be concealed,
Sometimes the wound of thirst cannot be healed.

The bustling breeze of memories traverse through the timeline,
But the eternal silence is truly divine,
The doors to the memories cannot be closed,
Sometimes the escape through memories cannot be secured.

My mother did not survive her last heart attack and took her last breath on 14 September 2014. Her husband felt guilty for days that he couldn't take her to the hospital on time, but he did his best. After her death, I used to get nightmares for months where I would dream of her having a heart attack and me being helpless to save her. I couldn't drive for days because my hands trembled. In those moments, my belief in God shattered. Continuous streams of tears erupted each time I drove my car. After her third attack, she was blessed with a grandson from her eldest daughter, and because of him, she managed to dodge death for almost 6 months since she wanted to live more for him. I was always right beside her each time she felt unwell, except for the last attack that caused her death. Once, I found her crying on the bed questioning who will rescue her if I am unavailable at that moment. Till the present day, I curse myself for not being with her when she had her last attack. Just a few hours before her death, she spoke to me over the phone asking me to run an errand at home and enquired about my health. To this day, that memory is clear in my head, as if I relive it every day.

The smiling face

The sunrays shimmering,
Wading through the misty morning,
Cannot be caged ever,
But it dwells in your lovely eyes forever.

The light from the orb of night gleaming,
Right on the ripples of water waddling,
Cannot be imprisoned ever,
But it perches on your lovely smile forever.

The water from the spring moving,
Falling on the rocks singing,
Cannot be cooped up ever,
But it nests in your lovely talks forever.

The unveiled bridal earth during spring,
With the heart full of love for every being,
Cannot be immured ever,
But it resides in your lovely self forever.

Well, I guess, after a while, you learn to live with that constant void in the life. Everyone close to her grieved in their own way, and some do so till this day during any important phase in their life. Seeing her photographs reminds us of everything she persistently adhered to for herself and others to life and how she insisted on enjoying every moment of life. She celebrated every day like it is her last day to live. Everyone in the family lost their light when she died because she was the energy hub that catalysed everyone's confidence to the next level.

My mother being an ordinary woman was a reason of happiness for so many people. No one can ever replace her, and yet, today, we try to be like her, an ordinary human being with extraordinary qualities.

04.12.1964 to 14.09.2014

www.ingramcontent.com/pod-product-compliance
Ingram Content Group UK Ltd.
Pitfield, Milton Keynes, MK11 3LW, UK
UKHW042001190726
13854UKWH00005B/2104

9 789390 034758